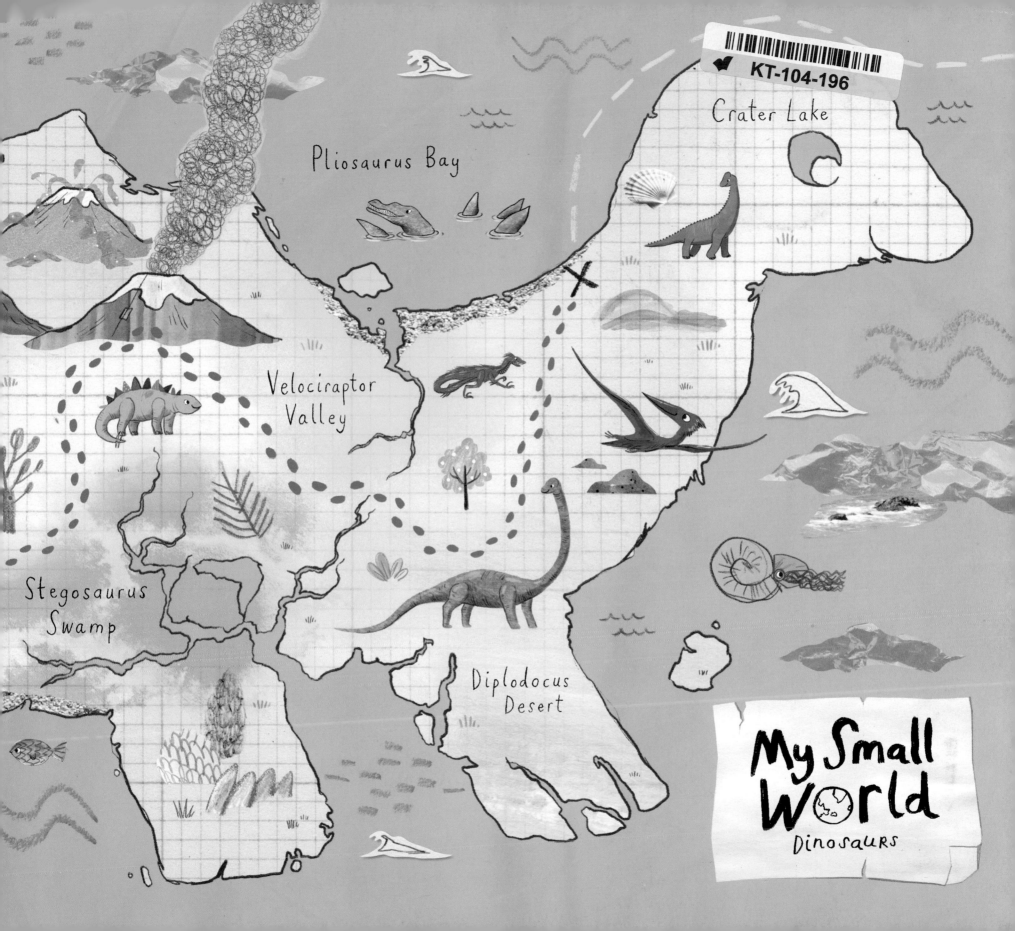

Crater Lake

Pliosaurus Bay

Velociraptor
Valley

Stegosaurus
Swamp

Diplodocus
Desert

My Small
World
DINOSAURS

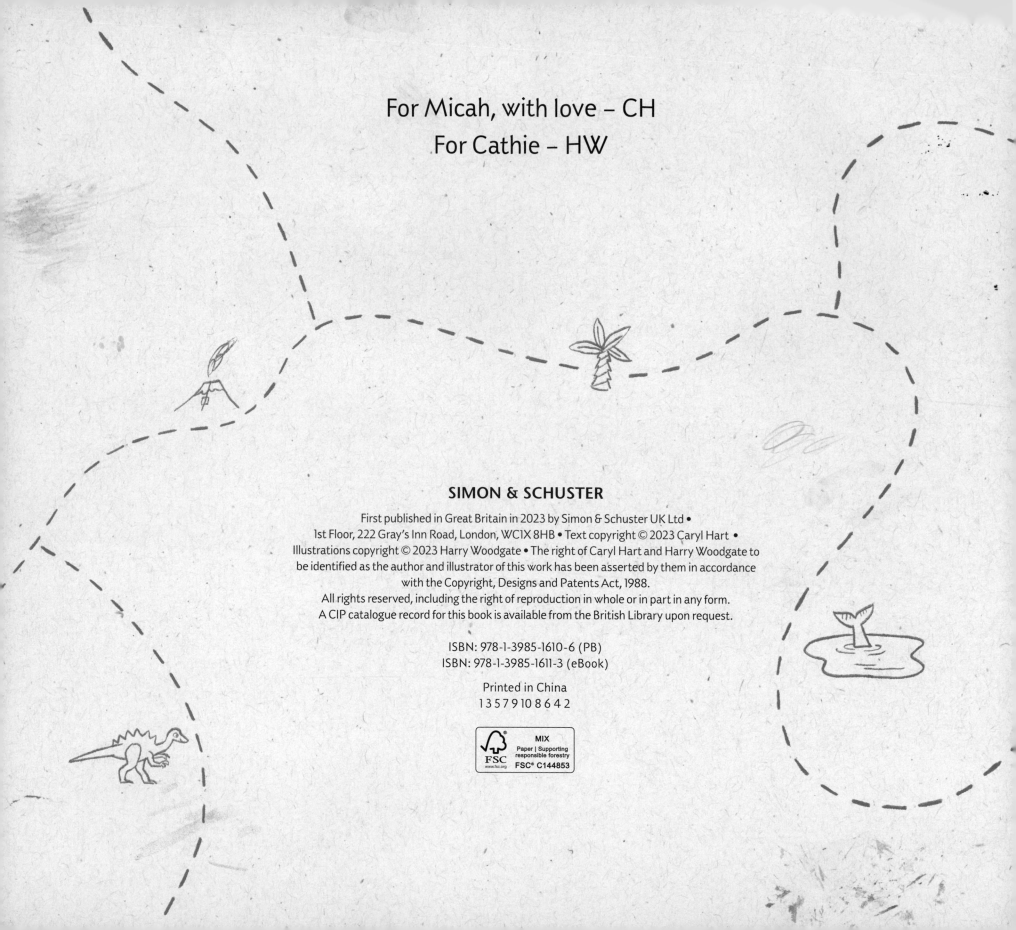

For Micah, with love – CH

For Cathie – HW

SIMON & SCHUSTER

First published in Great Britain in 2023 by Simon & Schuster UK Ltd •
1st Floor, 222 Gray's Inn Road, London, WC1X 8HB • Text copyright © 2023 Caryl Hart •
Illustrations copyright © 2023 Harry Woodgate • The right of Caryl Hart and Harry Woodgate to
be identified as the author and illustrator of this work has been asserted by them in accordance
with the Copyright, Designs and Patents Act, 1988.

A CIP catalogue record for this book is available from the British Library upon request.

ISBN: 978-1-3985-1610-6 (PB)
ISBN: 978-1-3985-1611-3 (eBook)

Printed in China
1 3 5 7 9 10 8 6 4 2

MIX
Paper | Supporting
responsible forestry
FSC® C144853

My Small World

Dinosaurs

CARYL HART   HARRY WOODGATE

SIMON & SCHUSTER
London New York Sydney Toronto New Delhi

Come close and I'll show you
a fun place to play,

Where creatures run wild
and the sun shines all day . . .

The treacherous sea's
made from shiny tin foil,

And there's cardboard volcanos
which bubble and boil.

Soft, cotton wool clouds
cross the crêpe paper sky

Where cute baby pTER-o-saurs
learn how to fly.

My small world is waiting, so come take my hand,
I'll show you who lives in my dinosaur land . . .

We'll start with some small ones, here's EUR-op-a-SAUR-us. These herbivores lived here a long time before us.

One hundred and fifty four
MILLION years
Have passed on the earth
since these creatures lived here.

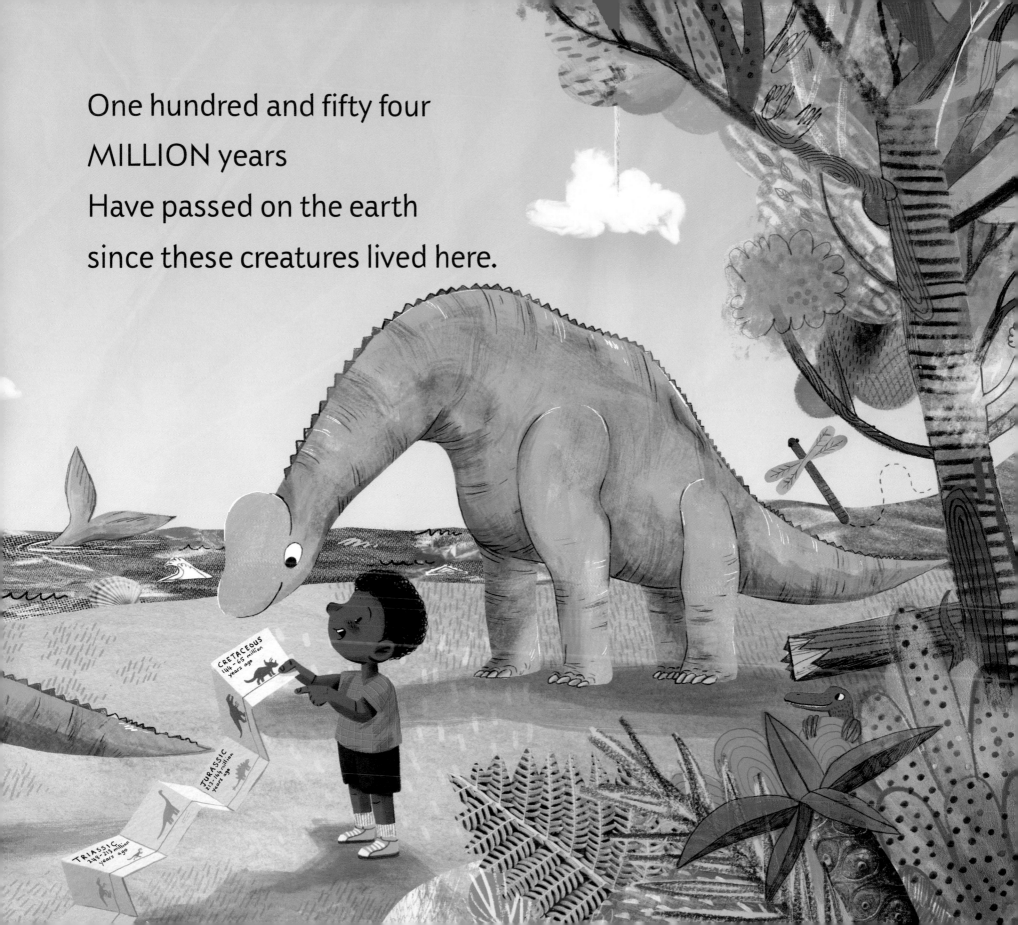

Way out in the sea
an Ich-THY-o-saur swims,
She looks like a dolphin
with flippers and fins.

But she's really a lizard
who likes to eat fish . . .

Let's feed her some bits
of her favourite dish!

But really, he's friendly
there's no need to hide.
Let's feed him some cake
and he'll give us a ride!

From deep in the forest I hear a great ROAR –
A carnivorous T. rex hunts down by the shore.

Stand still as a statue.
Don't hiccup or squeal,

Or that hungry T. rex
will have US for its meal!

Oh crikey, it's seen us!
Woah! Run away quick!
Now, hide by this log
where the bushes are thick.

Just look at those teeth!
This is not what I planned . . .

. . . But don't worry, you're safe in my dinosaur land.

Now, whose are these footprints that lead through the swamp?

A STEG-o-saur family
is out for a romp!

Catch-up, little baby –
there's no time to play,

Stick close to your mum
or you might lose your way.

Let's climb the volcano
to look at the view.

Look! There's a Tri-CER-a-tops
smiling at you!

And circling round us
the pTER-o-saurs fly,

A-swooping and soaring,
they flap through the sky.

Down there in
the valley are
beasts of
all sorts . . .

Spin-o-SAUR-us is hunting,

Dip-LOD-o-cus snorts.

The VEL-oci-RAP-tors are chasing their prey

And a huge PLI-o-SAUR-us swims out in the bay.

But . . .

. . . The warm sun is setting,
the day's at its end.
We must say goodbye
to our dinosaur friends.

And now it's your turn –
there is SO much to do.

Can YOU make a small world
for dinosaurs, too?

How To make your own Dinosaur Land

Ask your grown-up to help you along the way.

Fossils
Bury salt-doh or plasticine fossils to dig up!

Volcano
Fold some cardboard into a cone, then add tissue paper or newspaper lava.

Trees
Use a cardboard tube for the trunk, then cut some leaves from paper and stick inside the cardboard trunk.

Container
Try a large tray or shoe box; maybe an empty biscuit tin or even a cardboard crate.

Use all
your senses!

The possibilities
are endless!

More fun
= more mess!

FOREST
Stick real leaves into
salt-doh or plasticine to
create your leaf forest!

DINOSAURS
Use dinosaur toys,
or build some from
construction blocks or
fusion beads.

Water
You could try tin foil,
or a scrunched-up
blue scarf. Perhaps
even blue jelly!

DINO
crunch

GROUND
Use sand, cereal, oats,
rice or lentils.*

*Avoid using small pebbles or stones as
they can present a choking hazard.

Crater Lake

Pliosaurus Bay

Velociraptor
Valley

Stegosaurus
Swamp

Diplodocus
Desert

My Small
World
Dinosaurs

My Small World

Dinosaurs

THE JOLLY RAPTOR

X

Europasaurus
Forest

TRICERATOP PEAK.

Ichthyosaur Bay

Brachiosaurus
Plains

BEWARE!
T. REX

N

W   E

S